We're ... d all.

My name's Peanut!

... name's Floss.

I'm Sprat, her brother. (She thinks she's boss.)

...'m Finnegan. ...'s my bear. You can see him sitting over there.

We meet each week, in our shed HQ, ready to share our fun with YOU.

A
❧ *little* ❧
ADVENTURER

* IS KIND TO ANIMALS *
Even marching ants deserve
a lunch break.

* HELPS OTHERS OUT *
of swings, trees, hammocks
and even socks

* IS BRAVE *
Unless a monster is REALLY
scary or we get a splinter.

* IS HONEST AND TRUE *
PROUD GLOW

* DOES HIS OR HER BEST *
But isn't afraid to ask for help trying to
reach stuff which is really high up.

* LOOKS AFTER THE PLANET *
By treating it with ~~RISPECKT~~
~~RESPECKT~~ PROPLY

WHAT BEAR? WHERE?

PHILIP ARDAGH
ELISSA ELWICK

WALKER BOOKS
AND SUBSIDIARIES
LONDON • BOSTON • SYDNEY • AUCKLAND

It's time for a Little Adventure! Hooray!
Here are the Little Adventurers,
heading to their shed HQ.

What are they up to today?

IT'S ANIMAL SPOTTING

This is a chance for the Little Adventurers to find all sorts of animals in the garden. And to award each other sticky stickers!

I hope we find some fish!

The Little Adventurers get everything ready for an exciting day ahead.

"I've got my magnifying glass, to make little bugs look bigger," says Floss.

"I've got special fishy food to feed any fish we find!" says Peanut.

SQUEAK!

"I'm going to watch for birds with my bird-watching binoculars!" says Sprat. (He made them himself.)

Finnegan has a great big jar to put things in.

"Snub is keeping it safe for me," he says.

They start off the day in search of...

UNDERWATER ANIMALS!

"Let's look in the lake!" says Floss. She is *VERY* much in charge.

"No fish!" Peanut sighs.

"But look! A ribbety-ribbet!" says Finnegan.

Ribbet!
Ribbet!

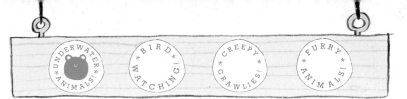

Floss has a staring-match with the great big, bug-eyed frog.

Meanwhile, Peanut – Oh dear! Oh dear! – has spotted a...

"OH, NO IT ISN'T!"

Floss shouts. "It's only a hosepipe."

"Phew!" says Peanut.

"It is a very *snaky* sort of hosepipe," says Finnegan.

Next, it's time for...  **BIRDWATCHING!**

Sprat finally gets to use his super special binoculars.

I may even spy a BEAR through these!

Finnegan spots a mummy bird with a worm in her beak ...

and the Little Adventurers follow her to her nest.

Wow! They've never seen baby birds before!

They look, but they don't touch.

CHEEP!
CHEEP!

"Our garden's FULL of birds," says Floss proudly.

"We even had an OSTRICH here once," says Sprat.

Suddenly, Peanut's eyes
widen in wonder.

She's spotted a...

"GIANT
EGG!"

"OH, NO IT ISN'T!"

says Floss. "It's just a ball."

"Well, it is a very *eggy-shaped* ball," says Finnegan.

"It's MY eggy-shaped ball," says Sprat proudly. "I've been looking for it for *ages!*"

Off again, and now everyone is hunting for...

CREEPY-CRAWLIES!

Sprat comes across a very friendly caterpillar.

"When you grow up, you'll be a beautiful flutter-by," he says.

You mean butterfly!

And look! Peanut has spotted a very spotty ladybird.

Why won't you fly into my jar?

Finnegan is looking for bugs where the tree bark is missing.

Sprat has his bugs in a bucket. Well, that's where he WANTS them to be. The bugs seem to have other ideas...

You tickle!

Finnegan is making friends with a worm as it eats through the soil.

Do you think he'd like to try your fishy food, Peanut?

No! I'm saving it for these ants!

Floss is carefully studying the map – *hmmm ... where to next?* – while Sprat looks for paw prints.

Uh oh! Finnegan has just noticed Snub
is missing. Now WHERE did he put him?

Suddenly Peanut gets all excited.
"Look what I've found," she
says. "It's a...

"OH, NO IT ISN'T!"
says Floss. "It just *looks*
BIG through my magnifying glass!"

Peanut laughs!

Even Pocket looks BIG next to this
speck of a spider.

It's teeny-
weeny!

Now the Little Adventurers are on the lookout for...

FURRY ANIMALS!

Peanut has found what might well be a mouse hole!

Look, Pocket!

Sprat thinks he might have found a real-live bunny!

(Hmmm. Maybe not.)

The others aren't sure WHAT Finnegan's up to...

Where are you hiding?

Then Floss spots ...
it can't be!
It CAN'T be.
It's...

"OH, NO IT ISN'T!"

Peanut shouts. "You said there are no bears in—"

"OH, YES IT IS!"

shouts Sprat, doing a little
My-Big-Sister-Has-Found-A-Bear dance!

It's hiding in that bush!

Sure enough, it is
a bear. It's Snub!

Finnegan gives the biggest grin EVER.

He hugs Snub.

Then he hugs Floss.

Floss is not used to being hugged.

She goes very pink.

ANIMAL SPOTTING is coming to an end.

What a day it's been for the Little Adventurers. What an adventure! Back at their shed HQ, it's time to give out the sticky stickers.

Everybody gets one, except Floss.
She gets TWO.

She gets the sticker for finding the
most important FURRY ANIMAL
of all: Snub the missing teddy bear.

And *another* sticky sticker
which just says:

THANK
YOU!

"See?" says her little brother, Sprat. "I TOLD you there were bears in the garden!"

WHAT BEAR? WHERE?

MOLE-HILL MOUNTAINS (Bumps in the grass)

HQ

And now they run around putting back all the animals where they found them.

N
W · O · E
S

THE LOST
PYRAMID OF BUCKETS
(somewhere around here)

X MARKS
THE SPOT
(where we
dropped
two sticks)

THE VALLEY OF ANTS
(well, at least TEN ants under a log)

THE NOT-SO-VERY-BIG SPIDER

BEWARE OF THE TIGER
(it's PODGE really)

BIRD
BATH
LAKE

THE BIG TREE

THE PLACE OF SHADOWS
(Actually Shadow's favourite place)

HERE BE
DINOSAURS

I wonder what the Little Adventurers will get up to next time?

Don't you?

little
ADVENTURERS
ANIMAL
FACTS

SPRAT's
BRILLIANT BEAR NEWS

- There are only eight species of bear.
  Not counting teddy bears!

- Polar bears have EXTRA FURRY bottoms, so they can sit on ice.
  Like thick trousers!!!

- Bears can stand up and walk on two legs like we do. That's because they walk on flat feet, not on their toes like lots of other animals.

- Most types of bear are VERY good at climbing trees.

- Bears have big brains and are intelligent.
  like me!!!!

- Bears have good eyesight, good hearing and an AMAZING sense of smell. They can smell food, friends and enemies from MILES away. *I would sniff out HONEY!!!*

FLOSS's
F-F-FEARSOME SNAKE FACTS

- There are about 3,000 different species of snake.

- They swallow their food whole.
  That's BAD MANNERS

- Snakes have flexible jaws so that they can eat things BIGGER THAN THEIR HEAD.
  If humans could do that, Sprat could swallow a water melon

- Snakes smell with their tongue.
  What a SILLY thing to do!!!

- Some snakes lay eggs, others give birth to live young.

- Although they may LOOK slippery, snakes are covered in smooth, dry scales.

FINNEGAN's
FANTASTIC BIRD FACTS

- There are just over 10,000 different species of bird.

  They wouldn't all fit in the bird bath!

- All birds have feathers, warm blood, and the females lay eggs. Most have hollow bones too (keeping them nice and light).

- Not all birds can fly. Birds that can't fly include: penguin, ostriches, emus.

  Unless a penguin is an airline pilot!

- Birds evolved from dinosaurs.

  WOW! I LOVE DINOSAURS!

- The bird with the biggest wingspan – across from tip of wing to tip of wing – is the wandering albatross with a span of 3.5 metres!

- The most commonly found bird in the world is the chicken.

  Perhaps she should HIDE better.

PEANUT's
ALL ABOUT SPIDERS

- There are about 40,000 species of spider in the world.

  I'm glad I didn't have to count them all

- All spiders have eight legs.

  Insects have six legs

- All spiders make silk but NOT all use it to spin webs. Some use it for climbing or for floating through the air (as a sort of parachute).

- An abandoned spider's web is called a cobweb.

- Some spiders are poisonous but most are harmless to humans.

- Most spiders don't have two eyes. They have many more than that!

  I wonder what a pair of spider glasses would look like?

ARDAGH & ELWICK

Award-winning author Philip Ardagh and author/illustrator Elissa Elwick teamed up as Ardagh & Elwick to create the Little Adventurers. Although Ardagh writes the final words and Elwick draws the final pictures, they work together on making up the stories and deciding what everyone gets up to on each page, which is far too much fun. Ardagh is very tall with a big bushy beard. Elwick isn't.

*To well-loved teddy
bears everywhere.
Often the greatest gift of all.
P.A.*

*For Martin,
My favourite Adventurer.
E.E.*

*The Little Adventurers series is dedicated to the memory of Sally Goldsworthy
of The Discover Children's Story Centre, Stratford, East London.
She was an inspiration to so many.*

First published 2017 by
Walker Books Ltd
87 Vauxhall Walk
London SE11 5HJ

10 9 8 7 6 5 4 3 2 1

Text and illustrations © 2017
Philip Ardagh and Elissa Elwick

The right of Philip Ardagh and
Elissa Elwick to be identified
as author and illustrator of this
work has been asserted by them
in accordance with the Copyright,
Designs and Patents Act 1988

This book has been typeset
in Century Schoolbook

Printed in China

British Library Cataloguing in
Publication Data: a catalogue
record for this book is available
from the British Library

ISBN 978-1-4063-6436-1
(hardback)
ISBN 978-1-4063-7712-5
(paperback)

www.walker.co.uk

MIX
Paper from
responsible sources
FSC® C008047